Lily's Story

J. L. Franklin

PublishAmerica
Baltimore

First printing

All characters in this book are fictitious, and any resemblance to real persons, living or dead, is coincidental.

ISBN: 1-4241-7822-3
PUBLISHED BY PUBLISHAMERICA, LLLP
www.publishamerica.com
Baltimore

Printed in the United States of America

ONE

On a Sunday morning in late May I sat at my kitchen table drinking coffee and watching a praying mantis sitting on a branch outside my window. At least she knew where all the good men had gone. She'd mated with them and then snapped their heads off.

I hadn't always been this cynical. Once upon a time I'd believed in romance. Like every little girl of my generation I believed my prince would come along and whisk me off to his castle. I'm glad we're not feeding that notion to little girls anymore. There are far more toads than princes in real life. We should have more stories that give female children a realistic view of their futures. Instead of expecting a man to come along and take them off to a castle, they should be taught to build their own castles.

My teenage years were still full of romantic fantasies even though my social calendar wasn't exactly over booked. However I did have a date to the senior prom with a tall, gangly boy with zits. At least, I consoled myself, I had a date for the big night. The lights in the gym were dim and it was easy to pretend to myself that he was material for a prom king rather than material for an acne medication ad.

After graduation, I still believed that all my troubles would be over once I found the one who would complete me. It never occurred to me that I was already complete.

My romantic aspirations didn't improve much during my college years either. While my younger sister was the belle of the high school I was finding plenty of time to study in college. My social life definitely didn't interfere. My only serious relationship was with a boy my roommate introduced me to in my junior year. Like her boyfriend he was what was known as a jock. If it weren't for his value to the football team I imagine that his academic endeavors would have ended. His name was Hal and he was good-looking in a muscle bound way. Our first date was to a school dance. My roommate and her current boyfriend had smuggled in a bottle of sloe gin and were adding generous amounts to our sodas. Eventually I threw up all over Hal's shoes. He was very heroic about it and I thought that after you soiled someone's shoes you owed it to them to go on a second date with them. One date led to another and we became a couple. To be honest I don't think Hal ever had an intellectual thought, but I kept telling myself that he was just a late bloomer in the brains department. I hung on until I could no longer deny that he was seriously lacking in gray matter. It wasn't long after that realization that we broke up.

I dated off and on in graduate school but no one made a great impression on me. Obviously, I didn't really impress anyone either. Eventually, I got my degree and became a school psychologist, although art was my real passion. Always practical, I chose the field that was most lucrative financially, at least, in the short term.

After getting my degree I took a job in an elementary school in a small mid-Hudson Valley town. Charlie was the art teacher at the school where I worked. Eventually he asked me out and things progressed from there.

Charlie wasn't exactly a handsome prince. At five feet six inches tall he wasn't a tall prince either. I was two inches taller than him. His adorable grin and his big brown eyes were what won me over. Also, didn't I mention that I liked art? He encouraged me to paint in my free time and praised my efforts.

Charlie was charming and very attentive and I enjoyed his company. When he asked me to marry him I gladly accepted his proposal. We were married in a simple wedding ceremony with family and close friends in attendance and honeymooned in the Poconos. My prayers seemed to be answered. As they say...be careful what you pray for...you just might get it.

Not long after we said our wedding vows my prince emerged as a frog. Now he was so nastily critical of my painting that I gave it up completely; but that wasn't what ended our marriage and drove me to leave him, nor was it that I was constantly picking up his dirty laundry and cleaning his whiskers off the bathroom sink every morning or even that he had the table manners of an orangutan. It was when I found out that he was teaching his student teacher about more than art. She probably could have found a teacher with better equipment to teach her. Anyway, after the divorce was final I had no regrets. Charlie left the district with his muse and all our furniture and I stayed here and went on with my post-Charlie life. Luckily, I was able to keep our small house.

Since my divorce nearly ten years ago I hadn't met any interesting men—not that I hadn't tried. I'd joined an Internet dating service called "Happy People." Meeting men on the web seemed easier than any other means of searching for companionship and a good way to get back into the dating scene. However I soon found that the profiles people put on the web weren't always very honest. One guy posted a photo that showed a relatively nice looking man in his mid-forties and stated that he was active and physically fit. When we met he was about as active and fit as a sweet potato and at least twenty years older than his photo. I might have overlooked these traits but he had the personality of a tortoise as well.

My next date was equally charming. He was a husky firefighter who enjoyed wearing ladies' panties under his uniform pants. I don't like to share my underwear.

Another date offered to cook me dinner at his home. The house was quite lovely and lit purely by candlelight. Later I found that he wasn't using candlelight to be romantic. Instead he was forced to use it because his electricity had been shut off for non-payment. Lovely.

My last date from "Happy People" was a guy who was thoroughly into feminism. He had no trouble at all with the concept of the woman footing the dining bill. However, I did.

Needless to say I wasn't too happy with "Happy People."

Disillusioned with Internet dating I gave up on it. Sometimes I went out with my friends for dinner after school.

Other nights I began stopping on my way home at Mike's — a small bar in town. It was easier to grab a sandwich and a drink there than going home and cooking for one. Also, it made the nights alone shorter.

It wasn't a place I was proud of patronizing but it was the only place within twenty miles that served food. After working all day I wasn't up for driving that far for a solo meal. As a plus, the place had an assortment of interesting characters to talk to.

There was Betts, an overweight single mom, who was waiting for the man of her dreams to walk into Mike's and sweep her off her feet. I feared that she'd have a very long wait. Her chances would have been better at Weight Watchers and she'd be healthier as well.

Then there was Wanda, an older lady who worked at the local Walmart. She'd slept with most of Mike's male patrons and lived to tell about it.

Ronnie was a local contractor who came in with his wife Tami. Tami was fine until she threw back a couple of Jack and Cokes and then she entertained the locals with bawdy tales of her sex life with Ronnie. Besides embarrassing Ronnie, who then vacated the premises, she gave us all more information than we wanted to know.

James was a surly Irishman who sat at the end of the bar and drank steadily until he became openly hostile to anyone around him. He was particularly out of sorts since he lost his job at a local home improvement store. He was working the late shift one evening when he accidentally knocked over a commode that was on sale. Rather than facing the music he stuck the pieces of porcelain back together hoping no one would notice. Unfortunately for him one of the stores video cameras had captured his whole performance. Avoiding eye contact as well as avoiding getting near him was the best way to handle this particular patron.

The barmaid at Mike's was a tall, angular "Nanny McPhee-ish" type woman with a long grayish ponytail and beady eyes overshadowed by a large nose and a personality that ranged between nonexistent and downright nasty. Her name was Jolene but the local clientele called her Jo. Usually I ate my dinner at the bar and, because Mike's sandwiches had plenty of onions, ate an Altoid afterwards before I left.

Jo, I learned, had a fondness for Altoids so I'd give her one too.

That was about the extent of our interaction until one night I stayed on for a few glasses of after-dinner wine.

As the night wore on some of the local men began flirting with me. A bit tipsy, I began flirting back.

Suddenly, Jo was up in my face telling me to stop flirting. At this point I realized that she needed more than an Altoid to sweeten her breath.

When I told her I didn't think my flirting was any of her business she ordered me out of the bar.

Later, I found out that one of the men was her husband. Since he was the type of guy that were a dime a dozen at Walmart she needn't have worried.

Feeling very indignant that she had banned me from the place I complained to the part owner, who also helped run the town sanitation company. When he sided with her I knew that he couldn't tell the trash that worked for him from the trash he sorted.

I started eating at home after being banned from the worst bar in town by the nastiest barmaid ever spawned, but I survived. I later heard that the only women Jo could tolerate in the bar were those who were sixty pounds overweight and over the hill as well. Since I'm tall and on the thin side she probably saw me as a threat. Plus, I'm often told that I look much younger than my forty years and not very over the hill.

TWO

Forget the bar scene. My friend, Carlotta, persuaded me to go to a local club with her one evening. Carlotta taught in the school where I worked. She's been divorced for many years and raised her son alone. In school she dresses very conservatively. Outside of school Carlotta is a mover and a shaker. She loves dressing like Charo and going to all the clubs. Did I mention that she also looks like a younger Charo…sexy and gorgeous? The night we were going clubbing she even came over to my small Hudson Valley ranch to help me dress in the appropriate club garb. This consisted of my tightest pair of black jeans, one of her low cut V-neck tops, and my highest pair of spiked heels. While I was still protesting the appearance of my—in her words— "hot" outfit, she began to pile my long auburn hair up into a tousled mass of curls on the top of my head. I feared that I looked like Xavier to her Charo.

"Very sexy!" Carlotta proclaimed in her musical Spanish accent.

With her blonde curls bouncing, and a determined look in her large brown eyes she grabbed her makeup bag and began to transform my face.

When she was done she pulled me in front of the full-length mirror in my bedroom to admire her work.

The person looking back at me was a stranger who resembled Peg Bundy, from *Married with Children*, at her raunchiest.

Afraid to hurt my friend's feelings, I smiled dumbly at myself in the mirror and mumbled thank you for the great transformation she had made in what I knew she considered my normally boring appearance. Now I looked like the "happy hooker."

With her chest filled with pride she handed me my purse and led me out the door to her car. As we drove towards the club I felt like the monster going for a public viewing with Frankenstein.

The name of the club was "Dreamers."

When we walked in it seemed to me like "Nightmares" would have been more appropriate.

The bar and the patrons sitting at it reminded me of the bar in *Star Wars*.

As I swiveled on my spikes to flee, Carlotta grabbed my arm and forced me up to the bar.

She ordered apple martinis for us and I grabbed mine gratefully. Maybe if I got very, very inebriated I would make it through the night.

As I took a huge gulp my eyes rested on the macabre crowd of people gyrating on the dance floor. Lights flashed and music pounded as desperate middle-age females vied for the attention of greasy looking older men. It was a circus of horrors.

There were a few younger men who were obviously looking for an easy opportunity to bed an older woman. When one of the latter danced up to Carlotta she danced away with him. Carlotta wasn't easy but she loved to dance. Plus she barely looked older than her partner.

I wasn't alone for long. Suddenly a small figure appeared at my side. Before I could gracefully edge away the figure asked me to dance.

Looking down, I saw a diminutive man who looked like a cross between Truman Capote and Pepé Le Pew.

Even without my spiked heels, at five feet eight inches, I would have towered over him anyway. Having bought and downed a second martini since Carlotta danced away I was getting a "what the hell attitude" — which is exactly what I said to him.

He whipped me around the room like a tiny tornado. When the music ended I herded Carlotta off the dance floor and out the door.

Unpredictably, my petite friend followed begging for my phone number.

"What do we do to lose Lautrec?" I yelled to Carlotta as we scrambled towards the car.

"Easy, muchacha," she answered.

She grabbed me by the waist and kissed me firmly on my lips. Then she turned to my little pursuer and shouted, "What do you want with my woman, little man?"

With a look of horror on his face my persistent admirer turned on his heels and headed quickly back towards the club.

I stared at Carlotta in astonishment for a full minute and then burst into laughter.

"What?" she asked. "It worked, didn't it? I guess your petite amour isn't into threesomes, no?"

As we drove home I realized that the club scene wasn't my scene either. Meeting men was becoming more effort than it was worth. As much as I liked Carlotta's company I told her places like "Dreamers" meant bad dreams for me. She looked at me as though I had two heads of overly styled hair instead of one.

"You just don't give things a chance," she murmured.

Things, I agreed, was the operative word.

Although my friends meant well, their efforts always made me feel even more of a loser in the game of love. My friend Stella, who was the principal of my school and her attorney husband, Brian, owned a lovely home in the Hamptons on Long Island. Their hospitality was wonderful, so when they invited me to their home for a weekend in late May I was happy to accept.

I stopped on the way downstate that Saturday morning and bought an expensive candle and a bottle of wine that cost far more than I usually laid out for a bottle of vino. The drive down was better than I expected on a Saturday morning, not much traffic. I sang along, in my off key voice, to the rock on the radio. In what seemed very little time at all I was pulling into the driveway of Stella's gorgeous stone house. With all the spring flowers in bloom it looked like an ad for *Better Homes and Gardens.*

Stella opened the door on my first ring looking more like a *Vogue* model than a middle school principal. Her long, blonde hair fell like a cloud around her beautiful chiseled features. She was dressed in a simple mauve tunic and white slacks. Brian stood next to her looking elegant with his dark hair brushed casually to one side and wearing a white polo shirt and blue dockers. My long drive left me looking like a model for *Goodwill* with my wrinkled linen blouse and capris.

After we exchanged hugs and I gave them my gifts, I realized that there was another person in the room.

"Oh, this is our other guest for dinner," explained Stella. "Lily, meet Brian's friend Roger."

"Pleased to meet you," I said, as I peered over Stella's shoulder at a rather portly version of Elton John.

"Same here," Roger said cheerfully.

We all went into the great room where Brian hugged me and poured me a glass of the red wine they were drinking. We all sat down and discussed the merits of the wine from a South African vineyard and agreed it was quite good. Brian had a great sense of humor. He made you feel like and old friend from the day you met him. The conversation changed from the merits of certain wines to the current political scene. Finally, Stella got up to go into the kitchen and check on the food she was preparing for dinner. I excused myself and followed her.

"You are not trying to set me up with Brian's friend, are you?"

I asked her. Stella had tried to pair me off before at a school function. It was a disaster.

"Oh, he's quite nice. Brian met him at his golf club a couple of weeks ago. He told Brian that he just broke up with his mate of ten years. We felt sorry for him and thought maybe you two might hit it off."

"Stella, I asked you after the last time you played cupid for me not to do it again. The last guy acted like he was doing you a favor by meeting me even though he was hardly a prize."

"Don't worry. Roger doesn't even know this is a fix up," Stella reassured me.

"Read my lips," I protested. "I don't want to be fixed up!"

"After what Charlie put you through you don't know what you want anymore. Not all men are losers like the guys you've met since. Finding the right one takes time."

"Frankly, I'm fine the way I am. From now on just leave my love life or lack thereof to me, okay?"

Stella just smiled. She thought when the evening was over I would be spewing words of gratitude all over the place. Right.

To be honest Roger was pleasant during the entire meal and didn't seem to have a clue that he was supposed to find me irresistible. However, during after-dinner liqueurs he began to tell me about his departed ex whose name was Joseph. He had more than looks in common with Elton. Brian's eyes popped when he heard this, it wasn't that he's homophobic, but because he suddenly realized that he tried to match his friend up with a person of the wrong sex. As for Stella, she quickly excused herself to go check on the dishwasher.

The rest of the weekend passed pleasantly enough. After this mismatch, I felt secure that Stella wouldn't be trying to pair me off for a while. Although Roger was a great guy, he certainly wasn't interested in me romantically.

The truth was that I would have loved to be in love but it seemed that it wasn't in the cards for me. My friends kept telling me that my soul mate would come along when I least expected him to. Well, it was going to be up to him to find me because I was tired of looking for love in all the wrong places. The men I fancied didn't fancy me and every man I had no interest in found me enticing.

One afternoon I was watching a segment of *Oprah* when she was talking to women who were engaged but had cold feet about actually saying, "I do." They feared losing their identity if they got married. Oprah admitted that was one reason she had never wed. When I thought back to when I was married to Charlie I did feel that at that time part of me had disappeared. There was a lot to be said for being single and able to be yourself. Too many women have lost themselves in the shadow of a man. Maybe the type of loving, sharing relationship I sought was just a myth. Come to think of it other than Stella and Brian, I didn't know too many happily married couples. Probably the reason they got along was because their lives were so busy they spent a good deal of time apart. From now on I vowed I would find ways to be happy on my own.

THREE

So here I was on this lovely spring morning envying the detachment of the female mantis. As I got up to refill my coffee cup the phone rang. Picking it up, I heard Stella's cheerful voice.

"Hey, Lily," she began. "I've got an offer you can't refuse."

Of course, my first thought was that she'd literally dug up another man to try out on me. No thanks!

This time, however, she wanted me to house-sit a big old house in New England that had belonged to Brian's great-uncle who had recently passed on. It wasn't an inheritance that Brian had anticipated or even really wanted.

Brian was too busy with his law practice in the Big Apple to ready it for sale. He preferred to wait until fall when his schedule would lighten up enough for him to take some time off to attend to it.

She said they'd pay all the utility bills. When I protested she told me that I was doing them a favor taking care of the place until they could sell it in the fall.

Plus, Stella reminded me, I'd always wanted to spend time painting seascapes and this house had a private beach right on the sea. This did entice me as ever since I'd graduated from college I'd put my passion for painting on the back burner. What an opportunity to turn up the flame this would be.

So, on a rainy day at the end of June I loaded my bags into my SUV and headed off to an escape from my daily routine. The drive was long but pleasant. As I drove, I felt the stress melting away. Funny how a change of scenery will do that to you. As I drove I marveled at how fresh and alive the countryside seemed. Spring and early summer were my favorite times of year. It was a time for new beginnings.

After I got off the inter-state I stopped for lunch at a small diner. Although the place definitely lacked ambiance the waitress was friendly and the food was good. When I got back on the road I was feeling very optimistic about the summer ahead.

I drove for several more hours. I felt very adventurous and capable as I got closer to my destination. I am woman!

Using my GPS I found the town of Piermont fairly easily. Quite exhausted after a six hour drive, I stopped at a filling station. No self-serve pumps here. After the young attendant was done gassing up the car I got directions to the house from him. Obviously Brian's uncle's house was well known, which wasn't surprising given the size of the town. Very small. Very touristy.

Following the boy's directions, I twisted and turned up cliff roads until I arrived at a private turn-off leading to an imposing turn-of-the century clapboard house overlooking the sea. I parked the car and followed a path to the wide steps of the front porch and turned the key Stella had given me in the lock of the wide front door.

When the door swung open, I turned the lights on and was surprised to see a very cheery kitchen at the end of a tidy hallway. Off to the side was an enormous living room with a large fireplace and an inviting looking overstuffed couch and two cozy armchairs. Beyond that I could glimpse a well-stocked library. Near the front door a wide staircase led to another level. The bedrooms I supposed were up there.

Although I had coveted the chance to spend the summer painting in a private place by the ocean, I had envisioned a house in great disrepair. Stella hadn't done it justice.

Though Brian's uncle had been close to a hundred years old when he passed, the house seemed to be in very good repair. I was pleasantly surprised. The old boy must have had plenty of help despite his, what Stella described, reclusive nature. From what she told me Brian was quite surprised to inherit the place since he had barely known his great-uncle. It seems that the old guy had traveled a lot. When he was home he kept to himself quite a bit even though he was born and raised in the house. In a way, I could understand how someone who was away from home most of the time would just want to settle in when they were home.

I stopped my thoughts about Brian's late great-uncle and retrieved my bags from the car. Then I surveyed the kitchen cupboards—the shelves were bare. It was lucky that I'd eaten so well at the diner. My stomach was still pretty full.

After the long drive I had been too weary to deal with stocking up on groceries at the local market. I found a tea kettle and retrieved the tea bags I had brought with me and proceeded to brew a cup of tea on the old but well kept gas stove.

Taking my tea into the living room, I sank down into one of the large armchairs and sipped it peacefully. When it was gone, though it was barely nine p.m., my eyes closed and I slept a deep and dreamless sleep in the cozy arms of the old chair.

The next morning the sun came in full force through the room's large old windows causing me to blink myself awake. Stretching as I uncurled my long form from the chair, I thought ruefully that my middle-aged body would need some time to recover from being curled so tightly all night. Even though people often mistook me for much younger than my forty years my body aches told me the truth.

I found a bathroom on the second floor, and peered at myself in the old-fashioned mirror over the small sink. My long curly auburn hair was in total disarray and my green eyes which were, I thought, my best feature, were puffy and not very alluring this morning. I splashed some water on my face and set out to explore the rest of the second floor.

There was a large window at the top of the stairs that let the brilliant morning sunshine in and also gave a magnificent view of the rear lawn and the path leading to the beach. Farther down the hall three doors led to three large bedrooms. One had been equipped with a fairly modern bathroom with a huge claw foot tub and a separate shower. I chose this one for my sleeping quarters.

After I had unpacked I laid out clean clothes and filled the large tub with water and bath salts. As I relaxed in the warm water I silently thanked the cleaning lady Stella had hired to make sure the place was habitable for me. It was a lovely old place.

Stella said Brian had visited his great-uncle as a small boy and found the house dismal even then. When they took a brief trip to Piermont to access it this spring they apparently didn't appreciate its charms. Their home was ultra-modern so I could see where they wouldn't find this house to their liking. Then, too, not everyone liked big, old secluded houses or the constant sound of waves crashing on the shore. I was one of those who did. As a child I dreamed of living in a big old house like this someday. Of course, in my dreams I lived there with a handsome husband who adored me and we filled it with adorable children. Well, at least, I was going to live in my dream house for the summer.

When I finished my bath I dressed in a loose cotton shirt and an old pair of white jeans. Although it was going on nine a.m., the morning air still bore a chill.

A salty breeze ruffled my hair as I stepped out on the large veranda. Not ready to explore, yet, I settled myself in a worn wicker chair and enjoyed the view of the not too distant sea. I felt the stress of my normally overworked life fall away with each wave that I watched hit the shore. Stella had also expressed concern that I might be too lonely in a strange place by myself but I already knew that I'd be just fine.

Later that day I drove down to town and bought groceries and cleaning products. The local market wasn't crowded but the elderly clerk moved like a snail. In fact you had to observe him very closely or you wouldn't have been sure that he was moving at all. When he finally finished cashing out my order I could hardly move either. Standing in one spot for that long allows rigor mortis to set in.

My next stop was the liquor store where the owner was a cheerful rotund woman who recommended some of the local wines to me. After I sampled a few I was in a much better mood. I ended up purchasing a few bottles of the local vino and was on my way.

While I was driving around I noticed quite a few people who appeared to be tourists. The town, though small, boasted many lovely shops obviously designed to attract these out-of-towners like myself. With the close proximity to the ocean it seemed reasonable to assume that many of these people with their out of state license plates probably had second homes here. I supposed as the summer went on there would probably be more and more seasonal visitors.

When I returned to the big house on the cliff, I put everything away and headed down to the beach. The path down was bordered with wildflowers and as I descended the rock path I was lost in the beauty of the moment. Before long I was on the warm sand heading toward the waves lapping along the shore. I hadn't gotten very far when I became aware of a strangely garbed figure heading towards me. My first impression was that it was a bald male in tiny shorts and a midriff shirt. As the figure got closer and shouted a piercing "Helloooo!" I realized that it was a woman whose skimpy reddish-blonde hair was scraped back into an extremely tight ponytail.

"Hi," I answered, wincing at the thought of the pain such an incredibly tight hairdo must cause. The woman winced back at me—which was also due to the tightness of her follicles.

"This section of the beach is private!" she informed me in a not too friendly tone.

"I know it is, but I'm staying at the Harrington house this summer. It now belongs to my friends and I'm house-sitting until they can clear their schedules enough to get around to selling it. Mr. Harrington was my friend's husband's great-uncle and he left it to him."

"I wasn't aware Jacob had any close family. We've summered here nearly every summer since we bought the house next door and other than the weekly visit from his housekeeper he had very few visitors."

"Actually, I'm not sure that Brian and his uncle were all that close," I admitted, "but he did leave him the house."

"Well, my name is Hannah. I'd like to stay and chat but my husband will be wanting to head to town to eat dinner at the Lobster Pot. I'm sure we'll be seeing a lot of one another this summer. Our summer home is the next house down the beach."

"I'm Lily," I muttered, "and I'm sure we will." Secretly, I was wishing quite the opposite as I headed in the other direction.

For the first two weeks that I lived in the house I barely left it except to get groceries in or go down to the beach to paint or to swim. The smell of the sea and the rolling surf had seduced me completely. The path to the beach was surrounded on both sides by fragrant wildflowers with their enticing smells. Sometimes I brought bouquets back to the house and put them in whatever receptacles I could find.

My new neighbor and her husband, Leo, a rotund man who appeared to be a decade younger than Hannah and jumped at her every command, stopped by to view the progress of my work more often than I would have wished. All she had to say was "Leo" and he came to attention like a frightened terrier. If she felt disposed to offer her opinion of my painting all she had to do was shoot poor old Leo a look and he would nod his head in vigorous agreement. He was well trained.

Though the house was large and old and fairly secluded, I felt very safe and content there. Also, Hannah and Leo seemed to keep a watchful eye on me. Perhaps they thought I was a suspicious character.

At nights, as I sipped a glass of wine and savored the peace and quiet of the house and the sound of the sea beyond, I would be overcome with an almost sensual feeling. It was the type of feeling one experiences while awaiting a very desirable lover to join them, knowing they are not far away. It wasn't an unpleasant sensation although it sometimes caused me to feel as though something existed just out of my reach. Something that might fill an emptiness deep within me.

At first I thought it was the start of early menopause that was much more pleasant than the hot flashes I had expected to experience. Then I decided I was probably just happily losing my mind.

Therapist heal thyself, I thought.

What in this lovely old house could possibly fill the emptiness of a life lived alone and childless? Although I was content with my solo life, there were times when I wished my marriage had given me a child. Then my common sense made me realize that sharing a child with Charlie would have been very difficult. Raising one alone wouldn't have been easy either. Still I had my regrets in the baby department.

Yes, a house couldn't really fill all of my needs. The only thing I could expect here was a summer of relaxation by the sea in a wonderful old house. With its weathered shingles and wraparound porch it sat majestically on its cliff like a wise old matriarch. In the mornings its large multi-paned windows sparkled in the sun like diamonds. At night the moonlight flowed in like water. For me, being here was enough.

FOUR

Hannah announced upon one of her strolls that she was having an impromptu dinner party that Friday evening and would be highly insulted if I didn't attend. Not wanting to deal with a disgruntled Hannah, I told her I would be over promptly at six p.m., the designated time for cocktails. Having been more or less a hermit since my arrival I thought a little social gathering might be just what I needed to give me a break from my strange affair with the house. Since the invitation came on Tuesday I didn't have much time to change my mind.

The next day, I went into town and looked for a suitable dress to wear to Hannah's gathering. It was a hot humid day and every dress I tried on stuck to my skin. They made me feel like a stuffed sausage. Of course each sales lady claimed that I looked like a movie star in the dresses they were pitching. Maybe they were thinking of Dame Edna. After visiting at least three shops I became so hot and irritable that I gave up. As I walked back to my car I passed a mother and her small daughter. When I heard the child ask, "Mommy, why is that woman's zipper open?" I realized that I was in such a rush to get out of the last store that I'd forgotten to zipper my jeans leaving my scant thong clearly visible.

Looking the child in the eye as I zipped my jeans up, I said, "The open zipper look is very popular where I come from." As

I walked on all I heard was a rather disgusted "Really!" from the mom.

When the evening with Hannah and company came around, I donned a simple yellow sundress that I'd owned for several summers and twisted my hair into a loose mass on top of my head in what I hoped was a classically casual look. In truth it probably looked casually sloppy. Slipping my feet into a pair of comfortable sandals, I grabbed the bottle of wine that I had bought for the occasion and walked up the front path and down the sandy path to Hannah's house.

Leo answered the door and guided me in with one hand and took the wine bottle with the other. Their house was as large as the Harrington house but much more impressive. The entryway was tiled in a creamy tile that led to a large room beyond. It had obviously been created by knocking down several of the original interior walls. It was a beautiful room that had French doors leading outdoors at one end. An enormous marble fireplace took up most of the opposite wall. The remaining two walls held banks of windows that looked out over the sea.

There was a small dog standing in front of the windows. On our way past I stooped to pet it. When it fell over, I thought I had somehow harmed the poor little creature and my face turned red. Seeing my discomfort, Leo started to chuckle.

"That's our deceased poodle Fifi," he informed me. "When she passed away at the age of sixteen, Hannah insisted that we have her preserved by a good taxidermist so we could continue to have her in our lives."

I could only wonder what Hannah had planned for Leo when he passed on. Righting the toppled Fifi, I followed Leo across the room.

There was a group of people milling around the parlor with wine glasses in their hands. Leo introduced me to them and tottered off to find Hannah. Most were other seasonal residents like themselves but there was a local realtor and his wife and the owner of a local boutique. The realtor was a red-faced jovial middle-aged man and his wife was a small weathered brunette. The boutique owner was a tall redhead, with amazing green eyes, who looked to be in her forties. Her fiancé was a tall, blonde man who seemed transfixed by her.

A heavy sixtyish woman whose bleached blonde hair was sprayed into a style that was no longer "the style," introduced herself as Joan. She had, she informed me, driven in from Boston that morning.

"After all," she proclaimed, "I'd drive anywhere to attend one of Hannah's yummy dinner parties."

Judging by her heft, I decided that she probably drove just about anywhere for a good meal.

"Yes," agreed a very thin middle-aged man who popped out from behind her as though he had been hiding there.

"Leo and Hannah throw such lovely bashes here at their little seaside abode!"

If he thought this place was a "little abode," I could only wonder what their normal lifestyle of this group was. Though low in weight the thin man was big on conversation. He kept up an ongoing conversation with everyone in the room but kept returning to my vicinity like a spaceship to its mother ship. When we were all seated for dinner and I found myself seated next to my satellite, I began to suspect foul play. It suddenly dawned on me that every person but Ichabod Crane and I were part of a couple. With the realization that Hannah was trying to make a match between us, I shot her a murderous look which she chose to ignore. I made the best of the situation and managed to continue small talk with the other guests while fending off advances from Ichabod whose real name was Archie. The real estate agent, Wilson, was very interested in what Brian planned on doing with the house. Although I knew he was planning on selling it for them I acted as if I had no clue.

The lovely boutique owner, Lori, was chatty and friendly. She told me she came to Piermont a few years ago on vacation and saw the possibility of bringing her clothing boutique to the area. It was a big success and she'd been here ever since. I didn't mention that hers was one of the boutiques that I'd visited in my search for a dress the other day. Turning the air conditioner to a cooler setting would have helped me from dripping on her wares. Luckily she hadn't been there at the time and another woman had helped me.

Lori introduced me to the blonde man, Harry, who was the local florist. They had recently became engaged and gazed at one another adoringly. Lucky them.

Although all of Hannah's dinner guests were pleasant enough, being paired with Archie wasn't. He was a nice enough man but definitely not my type. He was the local undertaker and informed me that if there was a call for a mortician he would have to leave rather than make a prospective client wait. Somehow the thought of being deserted for a corpse kind of unnerved me even though losing Archie for the remainder of the evening would have been a definite plus.

As soon as was politely possible I feigned a headache and, assuring my dinner date that I was perfectly safe walking the short distance home alone, made my escape. Personally, I would have rather been abducted by aliens than to have Archie escort me home.

FIVE

Forget the parties. I'm sure Hannah meant well but as I made my way home, I was silently cursing her under my breath. She was taking up where Stella left off. Every happily married woman seemed to think that their single friends were so desperate that they'd settle for any unattached male who was still breathing. Although I would love to find a compatible mate, I wasn't desperate enough to latch onto any available member of the opposite sex. I was determined to stay single unless I met someone who truly made my life better. I'd much rather sleep alone than with the enemy. I'd been there, done that. I plodded on home quite convinced my bed was destined to have only one occupant…me.

Once I reached the house I felt instantly calmer. Upon reaching my bedroom on the second floor, I quickly undressed and slipped beneath the soft comforter on my large inviting bed. As I gave way to sleep I had the vague sensation of arms closing around me and warm breath on my ear, very pleasant indeed.

The weather was breathtakingly beautiful the following week. I took advantage of the sunny warm days and had my paints and easel down on the beach early every morning. Even Hannah and Leo's daily visits didn't deter me. Hannah actually made an effort to cheer on my artistic endeavors even remarking one day that I might be another Grandma Moses with a career as an artist beginning in my later years. It took me a few minutes to recover from that one before I could thank her properly.

One afternoon another visitor strolled up the beach toward me. As he got closer I could see that he was a very attractive man about my age. In fact I had to force myself to appear to be engrossed in my painting so that he wouldn't notice me drooling on my seascape.

He was, I told myself, more than likely one of the well-to-do upper crust seasonal people like Hannah, Leo, and their crowd. So I was surprised when he stopped and asked me if I were a professional artist. Though I knew he was simply being kind, I thanked him for the compliment and explained that it was just a hobby of mine.

Instead of just continuing on along the beach he started a pleasant conversation. When I asked him where he was staying he said, "Not far away." Evidently, he was a year-round resident, a single one I learned happily. My resolve to find joy in my solo life was dissolving rapidly.

His name, he told me, was Jack. Somehow the name fit his rugged good looks. His dark hair, parted in the middle in *Great Gatsby* style, accentuated his striking blue eyes and lightly tanned skin.

How I would love to paint him, I thought, and he must have read my mind.

He asked if I ever did portraits because he wanted to have one done of himself. I told him I had been told that my portrait work was fairly good. He asked me if I could begin one right away. I assured him that I could as I wondered if it was to be a gift for a girlfriend.

Well, take what you can get, I thought. A few weeks of painting this handsome creature was better than nothing and, after all, I thought, hadn't I already decided that the single, free life was best? Yeah…right.

Originally I assumed Jack would want his portrait painted on the beach. However he asked that we do it up on the cliff by my house. That was fine with me as it meant hauling my easel and paints a shorter distance.

The first morning he showed up exactly at our agreed time of ten a.m. His dark hair gleamed in the mid-morning. His eyes appear as blue as the sky. Although I was a nervous wreck, he seemed very relaxed.

Setting up my easel, I felt like the spider with the fly.

While I painted he remained quiet and spoke little but when we took short breaks he was quite talkative. I learned that he had lived in the area all of his life and was a journalist. He said he traveled a great deal and had visited much of the world but always enjoyed returning home. He said that he found that living near the ocean gave him the peace he needed between trips. There was no mention of family and I didn't ask.

With each morning that I worked on his portrait I became more smitten with him. Painting his full, sensual mouth, I had to control the urge to leap upon him and kiss it. Something about this handsome, elegant man made me think of words like "swoon" and "vapors." When he left and I worked on my seascapes in the afternoons my thoughts were full of him. After my previous liaisons with the opposite sex, I kept telling myself to just complete the portrait and keep things on a professional level. Not that I had much choice anyway.

I realized that my infatuation, unfortunately, had to be purely one-sided. Although there were times that I thought he was interested by the way he looked at me, he always departed soon after his session ended. My offers of an early lunch were politely turned down. He apologized for being a very light eater who rarely took time for lunch. I got the message…this was about a portrait—nothing more…Damn!

Another day I was painting one of my seascapes on the beach when Hannah came up behind me and peered over my shoulder.

"Coming along nicely," she said pleasantly.

"Thanks," I answered, looking back to see Hannah dressed in a provocatively revealing top and tiny shorts. From the neck down she looked like Britney Spears and from the neck up my ancient Aunt Fanny, although my aunt didn't wear so much makeup. Hannah, I believe, was caught in some kind of a time warp. Since Leo didn't seem to mind I thought it was probably okay.

"You haven't been down here in the morning lately," she observed. "Have you been sleeping in?"

"No, actually I've been painting a portrait of one of the local people up on the cliff. He prefers to sit for me in the mornings. He probably likes his evenings to himself."

"Really? Perhaps I know him? What's his name? Leo and I know most of the people around here as we've been summering here forever."

Although I didn't doubt that I was curious to learn more about him, not only did I tell Hannah his name, admitting that I never got his surname, but I described him in vivid detail.

"I was certain that I knew all the local people but this Jack doesn't sound like anyone I know. Is he new to the area?"

"No. He said he's lived here all his life. In fact he said he doesn't live far from here."

Now Hannah looked really confused.

"Darling, I know everyone that lives nearby. There's no one who fits that description and I, definitely, don't know anyone by that name."

Normally, this information wouldn't have shaken me as much as it did, but I lived alone in the big house on the cliff. Without checking it out, I had been meeting a total stranger up there every morning. What had I been thinking? Right then I made up my mind to find out more about Jack before I finished his portrait which was nearly complete. He could be another Jack the Ripper for all I knew.

Strangely he never came back and if it weren't for the portrait, I would have thought that he had been a figment of my imagination because I couldn't find out anything about him. No one I asked seemed to have ever seen him.

I'll have to admit that rather than being relieved that he was out of my life, I felt strangely let down. After all what's a vacation without a mysterious and possibly dangerous man in it? Damn, I thought, I came here to relax and enjoy being alone and here I was mooning over some stranger who obviously lied to me about his identity and made a fool out of me by having me paint a portrait of him and then sticking me with it. I'd wasted three weeks painting a gorgeous stranger who was just playing head games with me. Not being attracted to me was forgivable. Going out of his way to make a fool out of me wasn't.

At least, the house seemed to like me. There were times when I felt that I really wasn't alone there. I would awake at night sure that fingers had brushed my face as I slept. Some nights the sound of footsteps in other parts of the house would bring me out of a deep slumber. Things would get lost and then suddenly reappear in the most unlikely places. Not one to believe in phantoms I began to fear that someone was playing with my mind. Perhaps, it was the strange Jack or maybe another equally weird local. I had heard stories of locals in small towns resenting seasonal tourists although in this area the tourists seemed to drive the economy. Why would anyone want to scare them away? Most likely it was just my overactive imagination.

Well, it was almost the end of July. I'd be packing up and leaving on Labor Day weekend. Nothing was going to spoil the remainder of the summer for me. So far I had several good paintings done and the salt air had reduced my stress. All and all coming here had been a wise decision especially since Stella wasn't charging me rent.

A free vacation house was still a great deal.

SIX

Forget Jack. It was time, I decided, to start sampling the local flavor. If I got out more my nerves would probably settle down. Painting was great but I needed to get out and around other people.

I began driving down to the little shops in town and browsing around. There were some surprising lovely clothes in those little boutiques. The price tags on them were high end due, I suppose, to the wealthy tourists who frequented the area. Once in a while I treated myself to an especially unique piece of clothing or jewelry.

The many picturesque seaside restaurants were also, in the main, on the pricey side. However, none of this stopped me from occasionally treating myself to a quiet meal at a quaint restaurant. Sometimes, I joined Hannah and Leo for a meal at one of their favorite seafood spots. I enjoyed their company but I often wished they weren't such picky eaters. They often sent their food back with complaints and when the revised dishes came back to them, I'm certain they'd received extra sauces. I hoped that my food hadn't gotten the same treatment. Although they offered to pay each time, I finally convinced them to let me treat them now and then. The more I got to know this eccentric duo the more I liked them.

Hannah and Leo seemed to enjoy my company as well. They invited me on quite a few little excursions with them. One time they were going on a large fishing boat that took tourists whale watching and convinced me to join them. It sounded like an interesting way to pass an afternoon so I happily agreed. When we boarded the boat, I wasn't really counting on seeing any whales because even the captain admitted that it was a matter of luck. Just being out on the sea was a beautiful experience. It was a warm, sunny day and the water was a brilliant blue. I was thoroughly enjoying the rush of the wind through my hair unlike poor Hannah who had her sparse hair fluffed out into an over-extended version of the flip. The large sun hat she started out wearing had long since blown off and every gust of wind restyled her hair despite what looked like lots of hairspray. Soon she resembled Big Bird on a bad hair day. I had to bite my lip to keep from laughing.

After we were out for about an hour someone screamed that there was a whale in sight. Everyone ran to get a spot along the rails to take photos. Even Leo took it upon himself to take part in the rush for a good photo opportunity. Hannah ran after him and managed to push herself into a spot directly facing the huge mammal when it suddenly lifted its tail and slapped it down hard on the surface of the water. A huge spray of water engulfed Hannah soaking her from head to toe. Now her overly teased hair collapsed into the few thin strands that actually were all she had. With her prominent nose and close set eyes she looked like a bald eagle. She held her sun hat over her head the entire way home. She was also very quiet and needless to say so were Leo and I.

On one of my now frequent ventures into town I stopped at an inviting bookstore that had an area with chairs to sit in and read. There was even a pot of coffee along with cups and sugar and cream. I couldn't resist such an inviting atmosphere so I found a book to preview and made myself cozy in one of the empty chairs. After a cup of coffee and a bit of a read, I decided to purchase a book. A pretty blonde woman about my age greeted me cheerfully at the register. She told me she had read the book and found it very interesting. During a brief conversation with her I learned that she was the owner of the shop and that her name was Beth. She was a petite woman with short, tousled hair that she kept pushing behind her ears. At five feet eight inches I felt like "Andre the Giant" as I towered over her. As I prepared to leave the shop, she asked me if I'd be interested in coming to hear any of the speakers the book club hosted once a week. It sounded like a pleasant way to spend an evening so I took a brochure listing the upcoming speakers and promised her that I would attend the next one.

At night, I was becoming used to being lulled to sleep by the sound of the waves meeting the shore. One evening, I partially awoke in the dead of night to what I would have sworn was a male voice whispering, "Lily," in my ear. Instead of being frightened I let a sigh escape me. Again, I had the impression of strong arms around me and feeling safe and secure, I slipped back into a sound sleep. In the morning I attributed my night visitor to a dream of the aging spinster I was becoming.

When the next book club meeting came up I arrived at the bookstore a little early and found Beth quite happy to see me. She led me over to the area with the chairs. She had just brewed a fresh pot of coffee and told me to enjoy a cup while I was waiting for the other club members to show up. As I took a Styrofoam cup and filled it with steaming coffee and cream a plump but pretty woman with bleached blonde hair tied back in a ponytail came in and placed a box of bakery cookies next to the coffee pot.

"Hi, I'm Abbie," she announced, plopping down in the chair next to mine. She said she was a teacher from Connecticut who spent every summer in the small cottage her parents owned in Piedmont. Now that they were getting on in years they seldom visited the cottage so she was able to make use of it for most of the season to just relax and regroup for the next school year. Her cheery manner and outgoing personality made me like her right away. Coming to the club seemed to have been a good idea.

The other club members soon began to arrive. They were an interesting crew. Laura was a stern looking, middle-aged woman with curly, white hair and a slender frame dressed in a flowered shirt and a long white skirt. Arden was an attractive redhead, tall, slim, fortyish, and obviously a city girl. Her stylish top and slacks were definitely designer and she was decorated with lovely diamonds and other precious stones. James was a middle-age, scholarly type dressed in light slacks and a button-down shirt. The last member was an attractive male, probably in his late thirties, wearing a tee shirt and jean shorts. His name was Joel.

After everyone was settled Beth introduced me and announced to the group that the speaker was going to be a few minutes late. The last book the club had read was a fictional story based on the true story of a serial killer. The guest speaker was to be a psychiatrist who had interviewed many of these predators to try and see into their warped minds for a book he was writing on the subject.

Eventually, a bearded man in his mid-sixties who had a very furtive manner about him entered the shop. He was the predator expert. Once he got into his subject his small, green eyes began to glow in an unpleasant way. I got the feeling that he might have some experience with his topic. I found his talk interesting but unsettling. When he was done and everyone had a chance to ask him questions coffee and cookies were served.

As I was pouring my coffee Arden asked me how I liked the speaker. Not wanting to seem negative I told her he seemed to be gaining a pretty good understanding of his subjects. She nodded her head in agreement and headed over to join Beth who was having a conversation with the speaker. I took my coffee and started heading for a chair. Arden gave me a tentative smile as I passed her so I stopped and asked her if the speaker had given her any insight into the mind of the serial killer. She said no but that might be just as well. We got into a conversation of sorts and I learned that I had guessed wrong. She lived here year-round and owned one of the small antique shops in town. When she was married they had vacationed here for a while every summer. When they got divorced she had just stayed on.

As we were chatting the fellow named Joel joined us. He was even more attractive up close in a blonde Viking sort of way. Arden introduced us. It seems Joel worked for the local sheriff's department. Somehow I never thought of deputies as the type to join a book club.

"How are you enjoying your summer here?" he inquired politely.

"Very much. I've always loved seaside towns. Also I love to paint and the Harrington house is a perfectly beautiful place to do it."

"It probably is. Old man Harrington wasn't big at entertaining guests so not many people would know."

Somehow I felt that he had decided that I was carrying on the old man's tradition of being antisocial.

The other members of the club introduced themselves as Arden, Joel, and I made small talk. Nora was not as stern as she appeared and had a delightfully dry sense of humor. She was a nurse who lived here year-round. James worked at the local community college where he taught history. They all shared a great love of literature.

Eventually, we finished our coffee and our conversation and headed out to our cars. We had selected a thriller to read before the next meeting at the end of July. I was looking forward to it. I was beginning to enjoy life in Piermont very much. Summer is summer…full of promise.

I drove back to the house feeling glad that I'd gone to the meeting. At home I'd never take the time to join a book club. Except for my attempts at dating, on-line and off, and occasional dinners with friends my post-divorce life was centered around my career. The lonelier I became the more I threw myself into my work. This respite was something I should have done a lot sooner.

When I arrived back at the house, I opened a bottle of wine and poured myself a glass. Settling myself in that big old armchair, I opened the latest book club selection and sipped my wine as I read. Thrillers weren't, normally, a genre I would choose. One of the great things about belonging to a book club was that you were forced to read books that you might otherwise avoid. Thus, your reading spectrum was expanded. Surprisingly, I found myself getting very interested in the book which was about a series of murders in a small town and was loosely based on fact. Vaguely, I wondered if Joel, the deputy, found it believable.

As often happened, I felt like I wasn't alone in the room. Damn, I thought, this book was really getting to me. I finished my wine and headed up to bed. No sense in reading on and feeding my nerves anymore than I had. I went upstairs and undressed. By the time I had my nightgown on I was already half asleep. As I snuggled down into the big, deep bed I sighed contentedly. Since coming to the house I had slept deeper and woke up more relaxed than I ever had at home. As my eyes closed I thought I saw Jack sitting on the edge of the bed. Wine and drowsiness can play strange tricks on one's mind because when I looked again no one was there. I drifted into a long and lovely sleep.

A few days later Stella called and announced that Brian would be away on a fishing trip with his buddies that week and she was coming to stay with me for a few days and bringing our mutual friend, Monique, with her. They were coming up that weekend. Short notice. Since it was her house I had no choice but to welcome her, although I was really enjoying having the place to myself. Plus, Stella was one of my dearest friends and part of me really liked the idea of having her around for a while. But, egad! Since I hadn't done much entertaining other than having Hannah and Leo over for drinks occasionally, I hadn't kept up on keeping the house especially neat. As soon as I hung up the phone I began tidying the place up. No small task. I had let the sink fill up with dishes. Clothes were spread all over my bedroom and the room I used for a studio was a mess.

By the time I was done getting the place in reasonable order it was eight p.m. and I was beyond exhausted. I ran a hot bath and poured a glass of wine. For extra measure I lit a lavender scented candle and poured lavender bath salts into the big inviting old tub. Finally, I lowered my tired body into the delightfully scented water and took a sip of my wine. Uhmmmm! Heaven. I closed my eyes and savored the quiet. Suddenly, I felt that I wasn't alone any longer. Although the water was warm, I was instantly frozen. I lay immobilized in the water. When I, finally, sat up and glanced toward the door I saw Jack in the corner of the room. Screaming, I threw my washcloth at him and watched as it slithered down the opposite wall. When I looked again he was gone.

After I calmed myself down a bit I called the sheriff's office. In a very short time Joel, from the book club, and another deputy arrived at my door. Wrapped in my big, old terry cloth robe I recounted how Jack had invaded my bathroom.

"You say this guy hired you to paint a picture of him and, then, disappeared? Did he have a key to this place?" inquired Joel's partner, a man in his early fifties with a buzz cut and no bedside manner at all.

"No, I don't usually give keys to virtual strangers. I don't have any idea how he got in." True enough, all the doors were secured from the inside when the deputies arrived. Since there were screens in every window that remained in place it was unlikely that he came in through a window either. Actually, it was also a mystery how he got out. The men had searched the house from top to bottom and no intruder was uncovered. No wonder they were looking at me skeptically. They probably thought I was lonely up here on the cliff and, having met Joel at the book club, decided to get him up here under the guise of a break-in. The fact that no one but me had ever met Jack made me look even more suspect.

"Are you sure you're okay up here alone, Lily," Joel asked truly seeming concerned.

Although I didn't feel too "okay" alone on the cliff anymore I managed to convince him that I would be fine. After they made sure that I locked up tight the patrol car disappeared down the cliff road. Shaken and feeling quite foolish, I sat on the sofa in the parlor and wrapped an old quilt around me. It was going to be a long night and if Lila and Monique weren't arriving the next morning, I would have packed my car and left that night. It wasn't long before I realized that I wasn't alone in the room. Turning slowly, I saw Jack sitting in the old armchair. When I looked again he was gone. I was losing my mind. After that, I collapsed on the old couch and fell asleep. That's how Stella and Monique found me the next morning.

"Hey, wake up. We've arrived for a long weekend of fun and sun." I blinked awake and looked up at Stella leaning over me as blonde, fit, and perfect as ever. With her long hair caught up in a ponytail she looked more like a student than the middle school principal she actually was. Monique, standing beside her, was equally lovely with her long dark hair pulled back from her face and secured with a barrette. Her mocha skin was glowing and her huge, dark eyes sparkled. She looked more like a fashion model than a successful city attorney. Faced with my two gorgeous friends I felt especially dowdy and rumpled after my evening on the sofa.

"Morning. I had a rather exciting time last night. A guy whose portrait I was painting managed to get in somehow and surprised me in the bath. I had the local law here but they missed him." There was no way I was going to mention the second visit by Jack. Even I realized that I must have hallucinated.

"Oh how terrible!" Stella was truly shaken. In her well-planned life things like that just didn't happen. She had always thought small towns were immune to things like break-ins. This one might well be because I was more likely just losing the cheese off my cracker. However, I wasn't about to share that fact with her.

"I would have been out of here, girl!" was Monique's honest reply. I admitted to them that the thought had crossed my mind but that I knew they were on their way here.

"Look, he's probably just a harmless kook. Let's make sure we keep the doors and windows looked at night and get on with enjoying ourselves."

I sounded more sure of myself than I actually felt.

Monique produced a small handgun she told us she always carried in her purse. She assured us that she knew how to use it and wouldn't hesitate if the intruder returned. Her self-confidence calmed me down and scared me at the same time.

While we were having our morning coffee the phone rang. It was Joel calling to make sure I was okay. He said he ran a check and couldn't come up with anything on any strangers in this area fitting the elusive Jack's description. Somehow I wasn't at all surprised.

Monique was just finishing her coffee as I hung up the phone. "Let's see what you've created this summer. With your talent as an artist I always thought you were wasting your time as a therapist."

"Yes," Stella chimed in. "Show us what you've been working on."

I hadn't really had anyone but Hannah and Leo over to see my work and they hadn't seen more than one or two of my paintings that were in progress when they visited. At this point I was more than ready to exhibit what I knew were some of my best works. Monique whistled softly when she came to the portrait of Jack. "That's one hot model you found yourself, girl. Does he have a brother?"

"What a babe!" Stella agreed. Then, peering more closely at the portrait. "He looks familiar. Have I met him?"

I hope not, I thought. Instead I told her that he was the creep who broke in last night. She didn't think he was such a babe anymore.

We were on the beach later in the morning when Hannah and Leo strolled across the sand and introduced themselves. Hannah was attired in one of her "Whatever Happened to Baby Jane" outfits. Leo, as usual, looked quite dignified next to her with a tee shirt and walking shorts. Opposites did seem to attract.

"We saw the sheriff's car over here last night. Was there a problem?" Leo inquired. I related the bathroom tale again while thinking it might have been nice if they'd came over and inquired if I was okay at the time. Jack the Ripper could have disemboweled me and they'd never had known until the smell wafted down the beach to their house.

"Oh, that's terrible!" Hannah wailed. "We've never had anything of that sort happen here before." I got the feeling that she thought I was a bad omen who caused crime to visit their privileged summer playground.

"Well, times are changing," contributed Leo. He didn't seem too ruffled by my story. Plus, he wasn't pointing the finger at me. I didn't entice the culprit to their area, I simply painted him.

Hannah hooked her clutches into Stella and Monique and instead of a girl's night out talked them into an alfresco dinner on Hannah and Leo's deck. Later, dressing in a long white summer lawn dress that I had purchased just for such an informal occasion, I swept my auburn tangle of curls into a deliberately messy bun and joined my guests (or was I technically Stella's guest?) for the trek over the neighbors. We were bearing wine and pastries and enjoying the sea breeze as we strode along arm in arm towards our destination.

As usual, Leo greeted us pleasantly and guided us out onto the deck where Hannah was entertaining a young couple I hadn't met before. The woman was rather exotic looking with wild blonde curls cascading down her back and clad in a billowing dress of sea foam green that matched her wide, sparkling eyes. The gentleman accompanying her was tall and slim with glossy black hair and a swarthy complexion. Visions of Heathcliff and his Cathy crossed my mind.

Hannah introduced the woman as her niece, Anastasia, and her fiancé, Daryl. They greeted us pleasantly. I picked up a bit of Boston in their accents. According to Hannah the couple drove up on a whim every now and then. Her niece had been a frequent visitor since she was a child. It seemed that she used to love spending summers with her childless aunt and uncle because they spoiled her as though she were the child they were never destined to have. As a teenager, they gave her the freedom her own parents denied her at home. According to Anastasia, she still felt freer here, at the shore, with her beloved aunt and uncle than anywhere else.

"Auntie and Uncle always encouraged my talents as well," Anastasia said proudly.

"What would they be?" inquired an ever curious Stella. *Fine, now we'll be subject to a piano or voice recital*, I thought meanly. Not that I would have minded a proper concert of any sort but attempts by amateurs were mostly insufferable.

Surprisingly Anastasia answered that she was endowed with the ability to see things beyond this world. Hannah chimed in and explained that her niece was a gifted psychic. If this was true I really felt sorry for her since I, personally, thought dealing with this world was hard enough. Stella and Monique, however, thought this was wonderful. They asked Anastasia if she could give them readings. I was relieved to hear that she didn't feel prepared to do anything right then but that she would be happy to come up and read for them at a later date. Between them they agreed on a date near the end of August. Great, one of my last weeks of peace and painting would be interrupted with guests. Although I loved my friends, I was beginning to covet my quiet days by the sea knowing they were going to end all too soon.

After last night's encounter you'd think I'd be glad to have company but since I was beginning to wonder if I imagined the whole thing I was less shaken.

Hannah served a lovely meal on her terrace. Anastasia and Darryl were interesting conversationalists and Stella and Monique were enchanted with the young couple as well as with Hannah and Leo. After dinner we drank wine and enjoyed the view of the sand and the sea. There was a light salt breeze blowing off the water and the night sky was ablaze with stars. As I sipped my wine and savored the night I knew the memories of this place would warm me during the coming winter. It was close to midnight when we headed back to the house. We drank another bottle of wine at the kitchen table then we all headed off to bed.

When the time came for Stella and Monique to return home the next day part of me wished we were all leaving together. As usual we had a great time hanging out together. They were going to help me close up the house when they came back for Anastasia's readings. That was something I was looking forward to and dreading at the same time. The freedom of summer vacation isn't easy to let go of.

As their car pulled away the big house loomed larger than ever behind me. Even so it appeared bright and cheerful in the yellow sunlight of the lovely summer morning. The smell of the sea perfumed the air. On the path down to the sea beach grass waved in a slight breeze blowing off the sea. I breathed in the salty air and vowed to enjoy every last second that remained of my summer solstice. No intruder, real or not, was going to ruin my fun in the sun.

The day was young but I really wasn't in the mood for painting. Instead I went into the kitchen, grabbed a beer and took it out to the porch. With a sigh I settled contentedly into one of the old, wooden porch chairs and let my mind wander. Maybe, despite what Hannah had suggested, I wasn't going to be another Grandma Moses but I was really enjoying having the time to put my brush to canvas. When I was a little girl I loved to draw and just assumed that I would grow up to be a famous artist. Then, as I got older I realized that very few of us are able to make a living as an artist. Eventually, I got interested in the workings of the human mind and became a psychologist. Working in a school gave me a guaranteed income and summers off. Although I had chosen the practical life, I continued to take art classes in my free time. When I was married there wasn't much time for painting. Since our divorce I hadn't tried to make the time until this summer. Even if I never painted anything grand, I felt proud of myself for finally putting what talent I had to use. This winter I would hang my works in my little house and relish the fact that I had produced them.

The afternoon was heating up and I pressed the cold bottle against my face. Maybe next summer I would do some traveling to exotic places and paint what I saw. At least, I was following my dream to some extent. Finally, as the day became warmer and warmer I headed into the coolness of the old house. Although the place belonged to them, Stella and Brian really had no interest in it other than selling it. Funny, because if I had inherited the house I wouldn't even consider selling it. Having a house near the sea had always been a dream of mine but homes like this were a bit out of my price range. Well, at least, I will have had this summer to live my dream. Too bad summer was rapidly heading towards its end.

As I headed into the living room, I took another beer from the fridge. Settling on the sofa, I pulled my feet up underneath me and took a long draught of the cold beer. Running around with the girls had left me a bit tired and it felt good to just do nothing. Sometimes being lazy is a good thing. As I let my thoughts flow I heard footsteps coming down the stairs. Since I was alone in the house I was either really losing my mind or very drunk on just two brews. Holding my breath, I continued to listen. The footsteps grew closer and rounded the corner into the living room. Then...Jack was standing in front of me.

"What the hell are you doing in my house?" I shouted. "You have one hell of a nerve!"

"Actually," he answered calmly. "You're in my house."

"Bullshit! This is my friend Stella's house. Her husband's uncle popped off and left it to her husband. I'm staying here for the summer as her house guest and you're a weirdo who broke in. I'm calling the police!"

I reached for the phone glaring at him all the while. Strangely I was becoming less afraid.

"Calm down and listen," he began in a condescending tone of voice. "I am Brian's great-uncle, Jacob William Harrington. I've lived here most of my life and for several months in my afterlife it seems."

"Right, and you look damn good for someone who was nearly one hundred when he kicked the bucket," I retorted hotly.

"It seems that we all return to our prime age after we pass on. As I aged well I looked pretty good right up until the end but this is certainly a big improvement. Unfortunately you seem to be the only living being who can see me. That's why I couldn't resist having you paint my portrait. I was glad to see that I'm as handsome a devil as ever."

"You're as crazy as hell!" I yelled as I took a swing at his smug self-righteous face. Sadly my fist went right through his face. Dang! This Jacob/Jack was a pretentious ghost. I fell back on the couch and took another swig of my beer. He looked at it longingly. I guess drinking was a pleasure he was denied in his new state.

"Since you'll be leaving at summer's end we can probably co-exist until then. At least, now I don't have to keep avoiding you. You don't know how hard that's been. At first, I thought you were the ghost. Takes awhile to get used to being deceased."

Thinking that I must be dreaming or insane, I tried to figure out why I wasn't frightened. Then, again, although Jack was annoying he certainly was back in his prime and made one hell of a good looking ghost. Also there was nothing particularly scary about him now. If he and his uppity attitude stayed out of my way maybe I could still enjoy the rest of my summer. Although this was Jack's house while he was alive it was Brian's and Stella's now and a great summer retreat for me. Jack wasn't going to ruin that for me.

"Okay, Jack," I said, "I guess we can share the house until I leave. By the way, when are you leaving?"

"Actually, you have as good an idea about my departure time as I do. Obviously, I haven't 'gone into the light.' I imagine one must hang around for a while before you go on. It probably makes the transition easier. What gets me is that when I was alive I never saw a spirit but you can see me very well." He did look a little befuddled.

"Guess what?" I snapped. "I never saw a spirit before either, except in a bottle, and I'm not sure I'm fortunate to be seeing you now. Can you please just vaporize and leave me alone."

Looking indignant, Jack left the room or to be precise vanished. I finished my beer and got another. Seeing ghosts gave me a real thirst!

When I was alone I got really scared but not by a ghost. The very real possibility that I was losing my mind hit me full force. In all of my not so short life I had never had a supernatural experience. Why was I having one now? Maybe, I reasoned, loneliness was playing tricks on my mind. But then wouldn't I conjure up a friendlier ghost than Jack? He wasn't exactly Mr. Personality. He wasn't even an entertaining haunt. When I met him on the beach and thought he was alive his physical appearance had captured my interest but now I knew he didn't even have a body. The fact that I had nobody either still didn't make me want to cuddle an apparition, not that he was the cuddly type anyway. Then, the thought hit me that I'd felt something embracing me in bed and saw Jack in the bathroom after my shower. The old lecher! Suddenly I was furious and he was one ghost I wanted to bust, figment of my feeble mind or not! Obviously, he thought he could do whatever he pleased in his own house with the advantage of his fairly new spectral state! This wasn't even his house anymore since he gave up the ghost. I had more right to be here than he did and a right to my privacy as well. Damn him!

A loud knock at the door brought me out of my angry reverie. I opened it to Joel. I must have been still frowning because he stepped back saying, "I just stopped by to see how you were doing. Being alone in a big, old house like this could get on your nerves."

It was apparent he thought that I was seeing things. Well, guess what? I thought so too but I didn't need it rubbed in. After all, a mind is a terrible thing to lose.

"Thanks for your concern but I'm doing just fine. There's a lot to be said for being alone. I notice you're not in uniform. Do you often check on the welfare of Piermont's inhabitants when you're off duty?"

"No, ma'am," he answered, looking a bit put off. "It's just that it's sort of secluded up here and I thought I'd stop by as a friend and a fellow book club member. I'd like to take you out for an early supper if you'd care to join me."

Although Joel was attractive enough and I had no problem dating a younger man, he really didn't have a lot of appeal to me. On the other hand, a night out with a decent enough looking guy and a free meal didn't sound too bad. Before he could reconsider his offer I said, "Why not. Just give me a minute to freshen up and I'll be with you."

In the upstairs bathroom I was applying lipstick and eye shadow when Jack appeared behind me. Whirling around, I confronted him with my knowledge that he had been in my bed as well as in the bathroom when I was half naked. With arched eyebrows he informed me that at the time we ended up in bed together, he hadn't been any more aware of me than I was of him. He, though dead as a doornail, hadn't yet realized that he didn't need his zzzzzzzs anymore. Perhaps, he countered, I was snuggling up to him. Furthermore, he went on, it seemed that for some reason, unknown to him, I had become able to see him whenever he was in a room so he couldn't be around for more than a minute before I'd be able to see him. Why no one else could was beyond him.

"Probably," I retorted, "because you're just my vivid imagination playing tricks on me." He looked at me as though he'd thought I was incredibly stupid. *Of course*, I told myself, *if I'm imagining him then I'd imagine that he thought that my saying I thought him up was inane.* My head was spinning.

"Hell!" he shouted. "I'm as real as you are and a lot more reasonable. Just my luck that my only heir, a great-grandnephew that I barely ever saw, would allow a silly woman to move in here before I've figured out how to move out! You'll be no help at all in trying to figure out why I'm stuck here instead of frolicking in the great hereafter."

"Solve your own dilemma. If I were you I'd be careful though as you're probably destined for a far warmer place than you're anticipating!" With that I snapped my makeup case shut and headed down the stairs. I ran into Joel who was halfway up.

"Sorry. I thought I heard you talking and I thought it must be to me since no one else is here. I was coming up to hear you more clearly."

"I wasn't talking to anyone. I was singing to myself." I began to sing a popular song from the radio in a very off-key voice while Joel stared at me strangely. As he walked me out to his red pickup truck, I chattered incessantly about how I always sang while I applied makeup. He didn't have much to say about that.

Joel drove us to a quaint little seafood place by the water. He ordered lobster and I decided on the shrimp scampi. We shared a bottle of Pinot Grigio with the meal. The conversation centered mostly around the book club and local history. Then we discovered a common interest in painting. He told me he had a degree in art from the University of Massachusetts and came back to Piermont to paint. When the sheriff needed new deputies he applied and got the job. Like me he let his passion for painting just become a mostly neglected hobby. As we talked I became aware of his expressive blue eyes and honey blonde hair. The fact that he was probably a good ten years younger than I lost its significance. As he ate his lobster, I couldn't help but focus on his full bottom lip. Thoughts of licking the butter from the lobster off that lip passed through my mind. Feeling like Mrs. Robinson, I tried to shake my lusty thoughts away. I nearly succeeded until we got back to the house and I invited him in for a nightcap. After I opened another bottle of Pinot we settled on the big couch to drink it. Before long I was feeling woozy since I usually didn't consume my wine in such large quantities. Handing Joel a glass, I leaned in for a kiss and into the cynical eyes of Jack who was lounging on the back of the couch.

"Damn you, get the hell out of here!" I screamed wildly. Joel, thinking I meant him, jumped up and headed for the door mumbling apologies as he went. Great!

"You needn't have ended your evening on my account," Jack told me with a slight smirk.

Too angry to speak I simply glared at him drunkenly. Picking up the wine I'd poured for Joel, I downed it in two gulps and, avoiding looking at Jack, I staggered drunkenly towards the stairs. Suddenly, I felt someone take me by my arm. Gasping, I realized it was Jack. Not only could I see him but now I could feel him as well. He helped me up the stairs, at least, I think he did. After that I blacked out and when I woke up in the morning I was in my nightie tucked into my bed. Go figure!

Rather than being grateful to my ghostly guardian, I was furious when I realized that he must have undressed me. On the other hand, I had to admit that in a way I was glad that my imminent drunken coupling with the good deputy was interrupted because today I would have undoubtedly regretted it. A common interest in painting didn't necessarily mean you should do the nasty with a virtual stranger. Funny how sobriety and daylight enable you to see such things more clearly. In some ways sharing the house with its original owner had definite advantages. If I could just be certain Jack did exist other than in my mind.

Later that day I had a revelation. I was searching my bedroom for the book club selection to read. When I looked under the dresser I found not only my missing book but also an old photograph. It was of an older man standing on the porch of this very house. The man in the photo was definitely Jack although he appeared much older. To confirm it the name Jacob William Harrington and the year nineteen ninety-nine was written on the back in a spidery script. Having seen this photo of Brian's late uncle, I now knew his ghost, irritating though he was, was for real. Unless, of course, I was losing my slim grip on sanity. After all I had made it through most of my life without ever seeing even a glimmer of a ghost. Why was I suddenly seeing one? What next? Banshees, witches, and demons?

Shaken, I made the big mistake of phoning my mother. Whenever I was feeling sad or anxious I had the habit of calling my mother and chatting with her. Somehow our little talks always made me feel better. However, at nearly eighty years old my mother had become somewhat hard of hearing and I'm not sure she always heard half of what I was saying. I knew enough, though, not to actually bring up the topic of ghosts or, if she did hear all I said, she'd think I was losing my mind. People in our family were not great believers in the supernatural. Unfortunately, she did hear enough to surmise that her oldest daughter wasn't feeling quite up to snuff. Before you could say ectoplasm she was ordering my younger sister, Nora, who lived at home since Dad passed, to drive her from her home near mine to the house on the cliff. Nora was probably bored being away from her teaching job for the summer because she agreed although she did persuade our mother to wait to leave the next morning rather than immediately. Even if she wasn't into driving here at a moment's notice Nora was a people pleaser and most likely wouldn't have had the heart to say no to my mother.

My sister was as easygoing as I was feisty. When we were kids I always made her do my bidding. Since I was five years older she looked up to me so when I asked her to run to the corner store for me she was happy to do it. I'm sorry to say that I often took advantage of her good nature.

Sometimes I felt that I was still taking advantage of Nora since she lived with and cared for our mom. My life was pretty much my own.

Although I loved my mother and my sister having them as house guests wasn't something I had planned on. After I hung up the phone I uncorked a bottle of Pinot Noir and poured myself a glass.

"Be careful," a voice warned me, "I wouldn't want to have to tuck you in again tonight."

I turned to see Jack observing me with a half smile on his face.

"Haven't you gone on to your great reward yet?" I asked him curtly.

"If I had you'd be very lonely tonight, wouldn't you? Instead you have the pleasure of my company."

Well, if I'm seeing ghosts at least he is a handsome one, I thought. To him I, asked, "What makes you such a great alternative to being alone?"

We bantered back and forth for a while and then we had a nearly normal conversation. Jack, I learned, had no more idea why he was stuck in his earthly home than I had as to why I was able to see him. Although he was born and had died in this house, he had traveled extensively in his career. He was, as he had told me, a journalist and said he had been to many other places on earth that would be more desirable to spend eternity in. He admitted to being quite bored before I arrived. As the afternoon became evening I became more and more comfortable with his presence. Finally, I told him my family, such as it was, was coming in the morning and I headed up to bed. In my dreams I was with a very alive and romantic Jack and I slept very well indeed.

Arising at eight the next morning, I blinked from the intensity of the morning sun. Making my way down to the kitchen, I brewed a pot of coffee and barely had the first cup to my lips when I heard a robust knocking on the door. Opening it, I was nearly run over by my energetic little mother.

"Hello, dear," she said, grabbing me in a huge hug. Behind her I could see my sister waiting to grab me in her own suffocating embrace. Finally, they sat down at the table fortified with their own steaming mugs of java. Hearing their light chatter about what was going on back at home did cheer me up. It was all so normal and I wasn't sure that's something I was anymore. Our little coffee cache was interrupted by a visit from Hannah who had probably seen my sister's car out front and, being nosy, wanted to see who I was entertaining at such an early hour. I introduced her to my mother and sister and handed her a mug of coffee.

"Glad to meet you, Nana," Mama greeted Hannah cheerfully. Nora quickly cut in complimenting Hannah on her latest fashion statement, a hot pink, off the shoulder tunic combined with a matching headband that held her thin, blonde hair straight up in a Don King tuft. The overall effect was of a large pink woodpecker.

Hannah assessed my waif-like sister carefully. Dressed in a plain yellow tank top and tan capris with her straight, strawberry blonde hair blowing in the breeze she looked adorable. It always amazed people that she had never married but she seemed content with her teaching career and an occasional night out with friends. At thirty-five she still had time to find Mr. Right and, at least, she hadn't ended up divorced like me.

My mother liked Hannah right away. After all she wasn't much older than her, although Hannah would never admit it.

Since they all seemed to get on well I invited Hannah and Leo to dinner that night. Their presence would take my mother's mind off of me and my problem which she would never understand anyway. My sensible sister would undoubtedly have me institutionalized if she thought I was seeing ghosts. Not that I could blame her.

In the afternoon, I took Mama and Nora on a tour of the town, stopping in each of its unique little shops. They loved them all. We ate lunch in one of the tiny cafés in town and dropped into the library before we left for home. Beth enchanted my mother and Nora. On the way out I nearly ran into Joel who was returning a book. At first, he looked a bit scared of me but I managed to cover my embarrassment over the way he thought I went berserk the last time I saw him. I introduced him to my family and invited him to join our little dinner party that evening. At first, I was shocked when he accepted but then I saw the way he was staring at Nora and vice versa. Well, at least she was closer to his age than I was. She was in another world the rest of the afternoon. She practically floated through the market while I shopped for the rest of the things I needed for dinner. Mama chatted away happily unaware.

When we got back to the house Mama went up to the guest room and took a nap. Nora helped me prepare for dinner. We shared a bottle of Cabernet while we peeled shrimp for the scampi and peeled vegetables for the salad.

"Are you dating Joel?" she eventually asked. I assured her that we were merely fellow book club members who had one disastrous date. I didn't fill in the details. Nor did I tell her about the evening he came by the house on official business.

Nora was very attractive and intelligent and she had her fair share of suitors. None of them ever seemed to suit her though, pardon the pun. After my divorce, I'm certain my poor mother gave up hope of ever having the grandchildren she so desired. Although I always thought I'd have children, I wasted my childbearing years married to a man I wouldn't have bred dogs with. If Nora didn't find a mate soon all hope would be forever lost.

I was more than a little surprised at Nora's great interest in Joel. Yes, he was very nice looking but so were most of the men who had wooed my lovely sister.

He certainly wasn't wealthy as some had been. He was intelligent and an avid reader though but she didn't even know that yet. Well, after tonight I doubted that their paths would ever cross again.

Nora broke into my thoughts by asking me if I wasn't bored living here alone for the summer. I had to remind her that I lived alone at home too. Of course, as Nora quickly pointed out, I had my job there and my little circle of friends to keep me busy.

I poured us each another glass of wine and we chatted about what had happened at home since I'd left. Carlotta, I learned, was seeing one of her twenty-five-year-old son's friends who was only twenty-eight. Although I preferred men nearer to my own age I mentally congratulated her on being brave enough to make herself happy and not worry about what other people thought. I'd have to call her and have them over when I got home.

A friend of Nora's had finally come out of the closet and found the woman of her dreams. Again I thought how lucky you were if you found someone that you loved who loved you back. I know, as I told my sister, that if I ever had the luck to find true love I would never let society decide for me if it was right or wrong no matter what the situation was. We clicked our wine glasses in agreement.

As I prepared the dinner Nora and I reminisced about our childhood and, generally, had a good time. The dinner hour arrived quickly.

The evening started out well enough. Of course Hannah and Leo already knew Joel. Nora intended to get to know him as well as possible in a short time. My mother loved being with people. Everyone was in a talkative mood.

When we had finished our salad and were starting to eat the scampi, my mother asked Hannah how long she and Geo had been married. I told her Hannah's husband's name was Leo. She still didn't hear his name clearly because she said that she was sorry that she had called Lana's husband Geo instead of Beo, pronouncing it like the abbreviation for body odor. We would have to look into getting her a hearing aid soon.

While I was sorting out my mother's hearing problems Jack suddenly appeared. He took one look at Joel and demanded that I get "Deputy Dog" out of his house. Looking at what must have seemed like empty space to the others, I muttered, "This isn't your house!"

Hannah, who was most in line with my stare, looked around her to see if someone was there. Then she must have decided that I was talking to her because she said, "Of course it isn't, dear. Our house is next door."

"Who's a whore?" asked Mama politely.

Joel looked ready to make another quick exit. Nora just gaped and Leo continued to eat like everything was normal. Realizing that I was the only one able to see Jack, I tried to make amends.

"I'm sorry," I told my guests, "I meant to say, welcome to my house because I'm so happy to be having this dinner with all of you!" Probably everyone but Joel bought my explanation.

Everyone went back to their meals and I tried to keep the conversation going. Jack stood by the wall glaring at Joel. Unfortunately Hannah commented that I was certainly a more sociable neighbor than old Jacob had been. With a disbelieving look on his aristocratic face, Jack countered that he was sociable enough with people who weren't always knocking on his door and watching his every move.

"Besides," he sneered, "looking at that atrocious hairdo makes me wince. If you pulled your skimpy white hair back any tighter your eyes might have ended up on the sides or your head. As old as I was I was younger looking than you until the end."

It was good that Hannah couldn't hear him. Then, to make matters worse, Leo said he used to wonder why the old boy never married and often wondered if Harrington was gay. Hearing this, Jack retorted that he'd rather have been gay than have to sleep with a folically challenged witch like Hannah for the rest of his life.

Joel changed the subject by commenting about how delicious the meal was. Everyone drank to that while I appeared to be drinking in the compliment. Actually I was busy watching Jack watching Joel again.

"You'd better be careful, Lily," he warned, "Deputy Dog is barking up your sister's tree. Not that I blame him."

"My sister can handle herself," I snapped back at him, feeling a twinge of jealousy. Then I was angry at myself for being jealous of a ghost thinking my sister was desirable.

"Yes, I'll bet that Nora's a good cook, too," agreed Hannah, obviously thinking that I meant that Nora could handle herself in the kitchen as well as I could.

"I've had enough of my dear neighbor," Jack whispered to me. With that he left the room pulling Hannah and her chair away from the table as he went.

"Oh, my God," shrieked Hannah delightedly. "This house is haunted! Something pulled my chair over here and I felt a cold draft."

Hannah had ended up halfway across the dining room.

"Why did you slide over there, Anna?" asked Mama politely.

The rest of the group just stared at poor Hannah. She pulled herself together quickly though. Her eyes gleamed excitedly as she declared that when Anastasia returned we would have to have a séance here.

There was plenty of conversation throughout the rest of the dinner thanks to Jack. Nora and Joel even used the chair scare as a reason to go for a ride after dinner since Joel thought she needed to relax a bit before bed. I was surprised that he didn't suggest staying in her bed that night.

When I was lying in bed later that night I had to admit that Jack had really been the life of the party. Also I began to see that he was a bit jealous of Joel which gave me some satisfaction. Best of all his little chair trick had proved to me that he wasn't just a figment of my imagination. I snuggled under the covers and fell into a sound sleep knowing I wasn't going crazy.

* * *

Pulling the chair out from under old Hannah was the most productive thing, I've done since I transitioned. At first I didn't have the strength to move a pencil. When it happened I wasn't even aware of the change at first.

One night not long ago, I had my usual evening glass of cognac and tottered off to bed. When morning came I had the feeling that I wasn't alone in my bed. Turning, I saw a lovely auburn-haired beauty on the other pillow. At first I thought I had gone to Heaven because this certainly had to be an angel in my bed. Then she opened her lovely green eyes and seemed to look right through me. She awoke and stretched her slender arms. When she got out of bed and went downstairs I followed her. At first, I thought I had a lovely ghost in my house. As time went by I realized that more than one night had passed and that I was the ghost. As the days passed I found myself intoxicated by the presence of this exquisite creature whose name I learned was Lily. To be so near her and yet so far away was very difficult. When I was alive I'd had many women in my life but had never found one I wanted to share my life with. My work had always been all I really needed. Now I'd found someone who enchanted me but wasn't even aware I existed.

At night I came to our bed and enclosed her in my embrace, though I knew she couldn't feel me there. I was the loneliest I'd ever been in my life. During the day I took walks on the beach often passing my neighbors Hannah and Leo. They hadn't a clue I was there.

Then during one of my walks I came upon the lovely Lily painting on the beach. She looked up as I approached and I realized that she was seeing me at last. Thinking fast, I admired her work and asked her to paint my portrait. I let her believe I was just someone who lived nearby. As the painting progressed I was amazed to see that I looked as I had in my prime again. When the portrait was done I realized that she'd be terrified if she knew what I really was, so I avoided her. She's, apparently, the only person who can see me. Then one evening we collided in the bathroom while she was bathing. I know I shouldn't have been spying on her but she looked so lovely immersed in those bath bubbles that I couldn't help but stare. The next time she caught me she accused me of invading her house so I had to let her know who I was. Our conversation wasn't very pleasant. I'm feeling things that I was never fortunate enough to feel when I was alive. I pray that sometime soon Lily will feel what I feel. Was this meant to be?

* * *

The smell coffee brewing and breakfast cooking woke me up in the morning. When I got downstairs my mother was serving breakfast to my sister. She saw me and instructed me to sit down and join them. Nora looked up from her plate of eggs with a happy smile.

"Thank you for introducing me to Joel," she said. "We really hit it off. He's going to visit us at home when he has a couple of days off next week. We had such a good time last evening."

"No problem, baby sister." I wondered if he had mentioned anything about my prowler report or that I freaked out when things started to get romantic on our date. Probably not, I reasoned, if he's smitten with Nora now. One could only hope.

After breakfast my mother announced that they would be leaving around lunchtime since she was having dinner with an old friend the next day and wanted to get home and be rested. I surmised that she thought I was doing okay on my own even though the house appeared to have a resident ghost with a penchant for chair tipping. As much as I loved Mama and Nora, I wasn't overly sorry to see them go. Without other people around Jack would be easier to tolerate.

Hoping Hannah wouldn't intrude, I took a blanket down by the water once my loved ones had gotten on the road back to New York. The sun was just strong enough to pleasantly heat my body and the sound of the surf soon lulled me to sleep. It was late in the afternoon when I awoke from my nap. The air was starting to acquire a chill. Stretching, I got up and dusted the sand off my legs and put my flip flops back on. I shook out my blanket and started up to the house thinking about what to make for dinner. Once I'd showered and changed into a lightweight sundress and sandals, I headed for the kitchen. Opening the fridge, I saw a bowl of leftover scampi from the night before. I heated it up and poured a glass of Chardonnay. As I was eating Jack came in and sat on the chair opposite me.

"I'm sorry for my rude behavior last evening," he began, looking truly sheepish. "I was jealous when I saw the young deputy here again because I thought he was your date. Then, I realized he was smitten with your sister. As for Hannah, she was always so nosy and watched my house like a hawk. Leo's okay though. Still I just wanted to scare her a bit. Very immature of me, I'll admit."

"Immature, yes. Scary, no. Hannah was delighted and plans to hold a séance here now. Her niece is a medium." Jack looked thoughtful for a minute then laughed a booming laugh.

"I remember her niece," he chuckled. "Little Anastasia. She used to have a boyfriend named Daryl. Thought he was a real cock of the walk, he did. A séance with those two should be amusing."

"Daryl's her fiancé now and they both seem very nice."

"I'll try not to disappoint them," Jack smirked. Jeez, a ghost with an attitude.

Jack kept me company while I finished my meal. As he talked about his life I realized that he was a lot like Nora. An only child from a well-to-do family he had a privileged but lonely childhood. He had had ample opportunities to marry but just never met anyone he wanted to share his life with. As an adult he had become a journalist and traveled too much to forge a relationship with anyone. I was taken with the sadness in his eyes when he told me how his career had been his life when he was younger and how in his later years he felt that when he retired from work he retired from life as well. That was something I could relate to. I reached out to touch his hand on the table and surprisingly, to me, it felt solid and warm. A small shock went through my body as I looked up into his beautiful blue gaze. I think this was meant to be. He stood up slowly and with my hand in his we went up the old staircase and into the bedroom. No one ever felt as real to me as my phantom lover did that night.

I left the house more infrequently after that night. Jack was intelligent, humorous, refined, and easy on the eyes. As they say—"Why try the rest when you have the best."

However, this didn't pass Hannah's sight unseen. She visited frequently saying she was worried that I didn't get out enough. Beth called to make sure I'd be at the next book club meeting which was supposed to be my last. Joel, who had a long-distance thing going on with Nora, had alerted her about my sudden reclusiveness. Obviously, news travels fast in small towns. When Nora called I told her I was busy painting when in truth I hadn't gone near an easel since Jack materialized.

Jack and I spent days learning about each other's likes and dislikes. We read books from Jack's library together and discussed them. We listened to music together. We walked along the beach together. We watched sunrises and sunsets together. We enjoyed just being together. I was the happiest I had ever been and Jack said he never knew happiness until he met me.

As much as I enjoyed being with Jack the whole thing drove me crazy. All my life I'd believed that if I was a good person I'd go to a better place after I'd passed on, but here was Jack, a good person, still in his house. Why was he here and why was I the only living person who could see him? I needed to talk to someone. Nora was definitely not a good person to tell I was consorting with a ghost. She'd have me committed before I could hang up the phone. Stella only saw things in black and white so she wouldn't be a good person to tell my little secret to either. That left Monique. She was raised in Jamaica and believed in the supernatural. Maybe she was the one close friend that I could confide in. I just couldn't handle this new turn in my life alone. She lived in Manhattan and besides her busy law practice she had an active social life so I prayed she'd be home the evening I finally got the courage to call her. Fortunately she picked up the phone on the third ring. After we chatted about all the normal things, I worked in the subject of my liaison with Jacob Harrington.

"Yuck," Monique sputtered, choking on the Merlot she told me she was drinking. "Stella said he was about ninety-nine when he went over. You must be one horny lady to be loving an elderly gent like old Jacob!"

I informed her that Jack was back in his prime and destined to stay that way while I was aging by the minute. Luckily, Jack's age at passing put Monique off more than the fact that he was a ghost of his former self. She felt that if you were lucky enough to find someone you really hit it off with than nothing else mattered. She agreed with Jack and I that we were just meant to meet. She felt that Jack had remained earthbound for a reason. She thought it might well be because he and I were destined to be together.

I felt better until Monique reminded me that it was nearly time to close up the house and that she'd be up with Stella and Brian to help out. Suddenly the thought of going back to my old

Jackless existence flashed through my mind but I pushed it away. She also reminded me that Hannah's niece Anastasia and her husband would be up to give readings. I told her how Hannah was arranging a séance at this house at the same time. Monique was delighted and said maybe then they could all meet Jack and they'd believe me. She had a point. I just had to make sure Jack cooperated. When I later brought it up to him he told me that he'd do me proud. We shared a similar sense of humor.

At the next book club meeting everyone was there except Joel who now spent his free time on the road to my mother's house. After we discussed the murder mystery we had just read someone suggested that our next book should be a ghost story. I was glad when that suggestion was overridden because living with a ghost was enough of the supernatural for me, although I felt that Jack and I were more of a love story. They finally decided on a historical fiction novel that looked quite interesting. When Beth asked if I would be there for the next meeting, I wistfully told her I'd try to be.

The weeks passed too quickly. Every day with Jack was more wonderful than the one before. Every night was intoxicating. Neither of us had ever known true romantic love before and we savored every minute of our time together. We only regretted that we hadn't met sooner and had been closer in age and were both alive and able to share a normal life. Looking at Jack, I knew we would have made beautiful babies together.

Nora called me every week with news of her progressing romance with Joel. As happy as I was for my sister I was also unreasonably jealous. Nora and Joel would be able to have a normal life, have children together, and grow old together. If I lived a normal life Jack would remain gorgeous while I grew old and shrunk up like the prunes I'd undoubtedly be consuming. Not a very pretty picture.

When Jack was near it was almost possible to believe that we were like any other couple in love. We laughed together and shared our days and nights together. He shared stories about his very proper family. I told him stories about my life with my very off-beat family.

Jack was easy to talk to, easy to love, and he loved me. We both took it for granted that we'd always be together. Surely the grand plan that brought us together wouldn't allow us to be separated again. Neither of us lamented about the lonely years we had both endured before we met. Here and now, we were together and that was all that mattered.

My mother was, of course, thrilled with Joel's visits and the blossoming romance and the prospect of marriage and, hopefully, grandchildren. On the other hand, a visit from my beloved would send her screaming into the night. Well, I was enjoying what I had with Jack and that would have to be enough.

Too soon, Stella, Brian, and Monique arrived to help close up the house. Anastasia and Darryl were at Hannah's planning to hold a séance at my house and Anastasia was going to give card readings afterwards. Hannah had them pretty excited with her story of the sliding chair at my dinner party. As for myself, I was becoming more upset at the prospect of soon leaving this house and Jack. I might just have to find a way to stay. I'd talk to Stella. Maybe there would be a way.

When the big night came, we all took our places around the big dining room table. It was around nine p.m. and the only light came from some candles I had lit in the middle of the table. Anastasia, with the flames of the candles playing beautifully on her young face, started with a prayer that only good spirits would come through to guide us. Jack, good or bad, was already there. I smiled at him as he stood behind Anastasia, ready to do his part. He smiled back. Neither he nor I had ever been to a séance before so we were playing this one by ear. We were like two mischievous children. Neither one of us ever fathomed what was about to take place.

Next, Anastasia began asking for whoever was haunting the house to reveal who they were to her. Jack obliged by blowing out one of the candles giving me a jaunty wink at the same time. Then, Anastasia asked if whatever entity had blown out the candle was trapped in the house, afraid to go on towards the light. Jack knocked over a small vase. Anastasia evidently took that as a yes. She ordered the entity, being Jack, to move towards the light. Horrified I watched as a protesting Jack moved towards a brightness that had appeared in the area of the house's old tin ceiling. He called my name beseechingly as he proceeded towards the light, seemingly unable to stop. I screamed, "Jack" and then I passed out.

* * *

When Anastasia started to direct me towards the light, I thought she was putting on a good show. Then, suddenly, the most amazing blaze of light appeared before me. As it became a softer golden tunnel, I felt myself being unwillingly being drawn into it. As I kept being pulled forward I could hear my beloved Lily screaming my name. All I wanted to do was return to her. Suddenly, the tunnel closed and I was on the other side. Lily, the is no Heaven for me without you in it.

* * *

When I awoke a beaming Hannah told me that Anastasia had cleansed the house of the spirit of old Jacob Harrington who seemed to have been hanging on. Brian and Stella agreed that it was a good thing since a resident ghost wasn't a good selling point. Monique, my confidante, came over and put her arms around me as I wept. The rest thought the strain of the séance had reduced me to tears. I never thought that Anastasia would have the power to send Jack into oblivion. Our little scheme had backfired and Jack, my love, was lost to me.

The rest of the group assumed that I'd fainted because the séance had unnerved me. Rather than make things worse, I let them hang on to that belief.

Instead of helping close up the house I begged Stella and Brian to sell it to me. Telling them that I felt like I belonged there wasn't far from the truth. I knew I couldn't leave the place where I, finally, found and lost love.

I arranged to sell my house in New York. Stella and Brian let me have Jack's house for far less than they would have sold it to a stranger. I quit my job in New York and opened a private practice in Piermont. In my spare time I painted and started to sell many of my seascapes during tourist season.

Without Jack, my life isn't as brilliant as it once was but I still have my family and friends. I gaze at his portrait and the memories sustain me. They have to.

Nora, eventually, married Joel and moved here. They are expecting their first child soon. My mother lives with them and has become great friends with Hannah. Hannah and Leo have retired and live here year-round now. I see all of them often.

Stella and Brian come for visits whenever their schedule allows. Monique visits when she can, too. She's the only one who knows that Anastasia's little exorcism banished love from my life.

I'm certain that Jack is in a happier place and that one day he'll return for me. Until then, I'll wait right here in our house by the sea. I can be complete on my own until we meet again.

Printed in the United States
90125LV00006B/290/A

9 781424 178223